PERILS OF PANDORA

Once upon a time, when the snow took over, witches and vampires from Thousand Winters migrated into the mortal world, transforming into half-human beings. There was still so much to experience and so much to taste for these creatures. They were waiting to be reborn!

In the heart of a desolate city lived Pandora, a half human vampire witch. With centuries of life behind her, with captivating beauty, and mysterious allure, she was the epitome of a femme fatale, but with a dangerous beauty not loved by all.

The city, with its maze of alleyways and towering skyscrapers, held a peculiar fascination for her; it was a place where she could lose herself amidst the anonymity of the night. However, it wasn't the city that captivated her thoughts on this particular evening; it was love. Despite being confined to her concrete tower, a yearning gripped her soul as she longed for her beloved. With a despondent sigh, Pandora whispered a spell into the night sky, releasing her yearnings into the darkness like a silent prayer.

She was not the typical vampire; she possessed powers surpassing those of ordinary bloodsuckers. Concealing her true nature and magic from humans while lurking in the shadows, she was aware that this set her apart as an outcast among many. Embracing newfound hope, she turned away from the window and decided to explore the world of on-line dating.

There are elements of reality that are beyond human imagination and science. And every creature that awakens craves love!

Her bedroom was her mystical sanctum. Her room was filled with scents of myrrh and frankincense. Her shelves overflowed with peculiarly shaped alchemical jars, her beloved "Narcotica" perfumes, and ancient 15th-century books.

DWARF MELMOTH

Melmoth was a dwarf blessed with extraordinary powers. He had a sexy twinkle in his eyes as if he knew the secrets to the heavens. Pandora's fateful encounter with him occurred amidst the ancient forest at Bar Lucifer, where they communed over the Biere de Sorciere, a tantalizing concoction infused with the essence of pines. In the present day, Melmoth had taken on the noble role of guardian to the witches, making his home in the mythical realm. His sanctuary was a wondrous cavern, its entrance adorned with a mesmerizing array of treasures—Lemurian Quartz, Auralite, Astrophyllite, and Seraphinite, all sparkling with an ethereal radiance that hinted at their potent enchantments.

He was an artist and a sculpturer; he suffered from an artistic lunacy, creating bizarre metal sculptures of insects and skulls such as Insectus Gammaticus, which he displayed at markets. He was known across the netherworld for his mastery of arcane arts and wielding spells. On the other side, Melmoth revelled in causing mischief and mayhem to all who passed, using his powers to play tricks on the unsuspecting public. He would make objects disappear and reappear, create illusions that danced before the eyes, and whisper cryptic messages in peoples' ears. But his pranks were never malicious; they were simply his way of bringing a bit of magic and wonder into the lives of those who needed it most. And though some mortals feared him as a trickster imp, others welcomed his presence with open arms, eager to experience the thrill.

But his greatest creations lay hidden in the depths of his cave; a series of magical mirrors that served as portals to other worlds, hung from the ceiling of his cave. With these mirrors, Melmoth and all the witches could communicate with the outside world and observe the lives of mortals and other creatures. Each mirror was infused with its unique enchantment, and it was also a means of interacting with Pandora in the mortal world. With a wave of his hand and a muttered invocation, one could step through the mirrors and into the mortal world, appearing before unsuspecting humans in a flash of magic. One such mirror he gifted to Pandora. It was crafted with ancient magical energies, saturated with crystals from the waters of Polynesia and incantations from the world time forgot.

At a glance, the mirror was ordinary at first, with a modest grey dull surface and an ornate filagree frame. But for those with powers, the mirror glistened with otherworldly holographic light, rippling like an alchemical silver lake, it opened a gateway into another reality. Pandora could step through the mirror and be transported to the magical forest of her friend and sister Kanuweia. A forest enchanted with lush pine trees, cerulean lakes, and succulent fruits where ancestral Pacific magic flowed through the air, where animals roamed freely on her land and spoke in tongues.

Despite Melmoth's diminutive stature, he possessed a larger-than-life presence that set him apart from mortal men. Pandora cherished memories of their wild passionate romance, recalling Melmoth as an ardent lover with a rugged edge. She fondly remembered how he would tenderly prepare pancakes for her, topped with fresh strawberries and cream, with his bruised and scarred hands as a result of his metal wielding. The essence of his character was not defined by the coarseness of his hands, but rather by the kindness of his heart.

Pandora held the mirror and the surface rippled, revealing the face of Melmoth.

"*Behind a mask lies another lie!*" he warned Pandora.

"*I saw her a few weeks ago. Randomly! She is travelling looking for goat keepers for her land. We met at Bar Lucifer. She seemed upset. She said, she has no friends, she feels lonely, and she has no man to love! That is so sad. Our Magical Unicorn!*" he cried out from the mirror.

No wonder Pandora could not reach her through the mirror, Kanuweia was in a long desperate search for good new workers for her estate. It was heartbreaking for Pandora to hear her to be in such distress.

THE BLOODY CORD OF FATE

Long ago, before online-dating, there was a man named Frederic. He was well-known in the town as an alchemist and a romantic poet. He stood at an impressive height of six feet three inches, with a well-built physique and a raw sexual allure. His chest was covered with a thick layer of silk-brown hair, earning him the rugged nickname "the Bear". His eyes were a charming shade of hazel, shimmering with green hues and yellow tones, depending on his mood. They were magnetic, promising a world of mysticism to anyone who dared look. He was very popular with women of all ages in his town for his poetry and songs. For as long as Frederic could remember, he dreamed of finding his true soulmate, someone who would accept him for the magical being that he was and understand his artistic temperament. He was Pandora's greatest love. They were two mysterious souls crossing paths, recognizing each other from their past lives. This was a divine union!

He opened the door to her soul and soothed her fiery heart. He would travel across the seas for two days by boat and journey one day by train without hesitation to meet her. This was a testament to her that if a man really wanted a woman, his desire to see her would transcend all obstacles and hardships. No matter what trials or tribulations life presented, he pursued her with steadfast determination.

Even though he was destitute, he would never fail to bring her little gifts as a token of his love, such as an expensive rare nail polish in the colour of Amaranth, a bouquet of hand-picked forest flowers of bluebells, Enchanter's Nightshade and sweet violets or perfumes from the village shop of his homeland-the smell of zesty Verbena and Lemon. His journey to Pandora was long and arduous, he braved many obstacles and temptations along the way, but in his mind, there was only her! And yet they were from different realms, their hearts still craved each other.

"My skin misses your skin," he would write to her.

And when Pandora had a bad day or a mood swing, he would lovingly call it the *"Caprice des Anges"*-the caprice of angels!

"I am here to show you what real love is and if I am gone remember me, and remember what real love feels like", he would whisper gently into her ear.

In his hugs, she felt her muscles loosen and her body sag, he cradled her like a cherished angel. In his embrace, all her woes lost their sting, and she envisioned an everlasting future with him. He would brush her hair lovingly and kiss her gently on the lips. With his tenderness came the passion. He would lay on top of her like a wild bear, his hairy chest heavy on her soft breasts. Her legs would wrap around him as he kissed her deeply, both of his hands cradling and stroking her face fondly. She could feel his gigantic hard cock rubbing against her, and she throbbed and longed to feel it inside her for eternity. He would pound her hard until they would both pass out from exhaustion and ecstasy. She could feel her insides being shredded with every thrust. Their lovemaking would be the death of them she thought.

"*Je t'aime, Mon Coeur,*" he whispered as he ran his thick finger across her mouth, her neck, over her nipples, and between her legs, then down to her clit and lips. He parted them as he leaned down and kissed her deeply. Then, he plunged his tongue inside her and licked her for hours. After hours of lovemaking, they would sleep for hours end and dream of distant realms, until it was time for dinner and wine; a dinner consisting of red meats, cheese, and wild fruits.

At times a peculiar transformation would overtake him, a haunting change would take hold of his eyes, and slowly they would become eerie black voids of abyss. They gazed fathomlessly at the universe his mind slipping into other realms. Those moments frightened her as he seemed less flesh, but more of a solitary mystical wanderer lost in the infinite expanse of time and in the heart of cosmos.

"*Take away the wine, for restlessness plagues me….*" He would cry out. In those moments she felt what it was like to lose him. She hoped it was not too windy for him in his stormy wood.

For a long while they lived happily together in passionate bliss, but the wilderness of his heart and the independence of his soul prevented him from surrendering fully to their love. It was late summer morning when she felt the emptiness of her bed. There on the pillow lay a note and a leather cord necklace which she gifted him:

"*I am sorry my love. The universe is calling. I must go. Please know your love has saved me. Goodbye.*"

As days turned into nights and months into years, she discovered the bittersweet taste of betrayal and heartbreak. She felt like a used-up muse for his poetry. Her love was sacred, but his love was bullshit. Three more years would pass until their paths would cross again, but Frederic had already given his heart to another, a young sea nymph Sofia, they resided on a distant shore surrounded by ocean and dunes.

"My true love Pandora has returned!" he bellowed to Sofia.

"Come back to me, I have cut ties with Sofia, I do not have the same affection for her as I have for you. I have told her about our love", he told Pandora.

Pandora agreed to meet him with caution and happiness. The day before she was due to be reunited with him, he changed his mind. He told her he could not cope with the intensity of their love. He needed serenity in his life. He needed silence. He needed simplicity. He needed Sofia.

The knowledge of this treachery ignited a storm in her soul she never felt before. She was driven by a severe desire for vengeance! That night holding a faded photo of her beloved Fredric, surrounded by flickering black and red candles, she prepared her curse. A curse to match her agony. She visualised his life force to red thick cord and whispered the final words of ancient incantation. A rush of powerful malevolent energy surged through her body taking flight into the black night sky towards him. She cursed him thrice, for him to feel profound pain and torment as he has caused her and inflicted upon her heart.

The following afternoon, awakening from her "love craze" she regretted her actions, but the deed was done, and the curse could not be reversed.

Suddenly a vision of Frederic appeared to her, his spirit weary and his heart enclosed in chains, he was gasping for breath. In her head she heard his voice, in her chest she felt a spear. The vision grew more vivid by the minute, now replaced with a red-blooded cord stringing her deeper into the void.

"No! Can you hear me?" She screamed.

"Hold out your hand, can you feel me?!" She screamed desperately.

She watched in horror as the red cord began to strain and fray, each fibre snapping one by one dripping with blood. The cord, his life force, was disintegrating, and with it so was he.

She was drenched in cold sweat; her heart was numb her eyes white with fear. The storm outside has not abated, instead, it has intensified, thunder roared like a wild enraged beast as if the devil was calling her. She knew that she had overstepped into the dark side of Black Magic. Satan was there that night and Satan was calling himself God.

She clutched her silk bedsheets, her mind still reeling from the vividness of her vision. The sense of loss and dread lingered in her heart and in her mind, she knew that he was dead. Panic surged through her blood as she grabbed her magic mirror, frantically searching for any signs of him in other realms. She called out his name with a trembling voice, but there was nothing. He was gone forever, in flesh and spirit. She has never felt more heartbroken or so lost, so utterly alone.

As seasons changed and new species of flowers blossomed, the world marched onwards, but Pandora was forever trapped in her guilt and sadness. She watched from the distance his girlfriend Sofia moving on swiftly, finding solace with a village musician and bar owner. She watched Sofia's new life unfold, a life in which Frederic's memory has been erased with new smiles and affection. Pandora from that moment knew that her love for Frederic was the purest one and in the heart of midnight, when she waited for lost souls to ask her which way to pass, she hoped that one night it would be him, Frederic.

Hundred years have passed since, she was still hopeful that one day his spirit would send her a sign or cryptic message and that one day they could both forgive each other. With a bitter-sweet melancholy, she knew that he would always be with her, bound by the crimson cord that connected their souls for all eternity.

THE CATHAR CASTLE AND FRENCH KISSES

From her bedroom window, she gazed out at the cityscape which seemed eerily quiet, almost lifeless, as if it had been drenched in a downpour of fear and decay. The only source of vivid light emanated from the neon signs adorning the bars and shops. The atmosphere was permeated with a sense of dampness and desolation, far from the natural beauty she yearned for. Faint police sirens wailed in the distance, their mournful sound merging with the mist intensifying the feeling of despair. Just then, a glimmer of hope brushed against her as she received a message from Jean on a dating website.

Jean was a tall and humble soul who resided in the village of Pau in the foothills of the Pyrenees. He was a modest and sweet French man with a heart of gold. Unlike the flashy suitors she had encountered before, Jean had a quiet confidence and genuine kindness that captured her attention. He described the scenery of his village as nothing short of spectacular, with breathtaking views of the mountain range and its proximity to ancient castles. For their first date, Jean surprised her with a romantic road trip adventure to explore the Cathar castles nestled in the rugged hills of southern France. His choice touched her deeply, as this was a dream trip she had shared with her late beloved Frederic.

Pandora carefully coordinated a meeting with Jean in a nearby town, where her trusted friend Kanuweia would serve as her chaperone. Pandora felt uncomfortable meeting strangers in unfamiliar territory alone. With great dedication, Jean drove two-hours from his village to meet her. The meeting was set for midnight outside the House of Justice building, which stood adjacent to Kanuweia's second grand mansion.

The moon was bright, but it was still dark out, and the autumn mist had made it seem even darker. Kanuweia was sent to inspect him first. She approached him with an air of suspicion, moving gracefully like a spectral apparition. She was draped in a flowing outfit crafted from soft pink ostrich feathers, and a striking necklace made of bird bones adorned her neck. Her hair resembled the deep hue of a raven's eye, and her eyes shimmered like radiant green emeralds, revealing a hint of suspicion as she scrutinized him. In one hand, she wielded a towering staff, while the other extended in front of her. With a captivating smile, she greeted him.

"Enchante! Come, Pandora awaits your arrival. I've prepared tea."

Jean looked petrified but proved to be a good obedient slave, following her inside the mansion. After tea and cream cakes, they drove to their desired location to rest for the night. Pandora rented a cozy little apartment with a jacuzzi in the middle of the bedroom and a giant bed. That night he was too shy to undress and get into bed with her. It was endearing!

The next day, it was a brisk autumn morning as the sun rose above the horizon, casting the world in a warm, orange glow. The crisp air carried with it a hint of wood smoke, and cinnamon, and the rustling golden leaves scuttled across the cobbled streets. People hurried out from their homes for their bread and morning coffee, their breath forming little clouds in the air as they laughed and chatted.

As Jean drove her through winding country roads, he delighted Pandora with tales of knights and kings, his passion for history shining through. She found herself drawn to his intellect and humility, feeling a familiar connection Their journey led them to a secluded hillside overlooking one of the ancient castles. With the rain pouring heavily around them, Jean unveiled a surprise picnic spread, complete with pink French cheese and champagne! Underneath a large umbrella and the stormy skies, he shared stories of the Cathars and their plight, the gentle patter of raindrops on their champagne flutes only added to the enchantment of that romantic moment.

Under the rain he sang to her the Middle Ages traditional Occitan song:

"Quand lo boier ven de laurar

When the ploughman returns from ploughing

Planta son agulhada

He plants his cattle prod

A*E*I*O*U

Troba sa femna al pe del fuoc

He finds his wife at the foot of the fire

Tota desconsolada

Completely inconsolable

A*E*I*O*U

Se n'es malauta digas-o

If you are sad, then tell me

Te farai un potage

I'll make you a stew

A*E*I*O*U

Amb una raba, amb un caulet

With a turnip, with a cabbage

una lauseta magra

and a skinny lark

A*E*I*O*U

Quand serai morta enterratz-me

When I am dead bury me

Al pus prigond de la cava
In the deepest part of the cave

A*E*I*O*U

Los pes virats a la paret
My feet towards the wall

Lo cap jos la canela
My head in the path of the water

A*E*I*O*U

E los romius que passaran
The pilgrims that will pass by

Prendran d'aiga senhada
Will take from the holy water.

A*E*I*O*U

E diran "Qual es mort aici?"

And they will ask "Who died here?"

Aquo es la paura Joana

Here lies the poor Joanne

A*E*I*O*U

Se n'es anada al paradis

She went to paradise

Al cel ambe sas cabras.

To heaven with her goats.

A*E*I*O*U

As the rain intensified, they returned to their apartment to seek shelter. There was now a new flutter of excitement at the prospect of being alone and naked together under the warmth of a duvet. His kisses were sweet and affectionate, he bathed her tenderly in the jacuzzi, washing her hair and massaging her shoulders. Under flickering candlelight, they made love with tenderness and newfound intimacy and spent the night in each other's arms. As they lay entangled in each other's arms, the rain raged on outside, but within the safety of their embrace, Pandora found a familiar solace and contentment. Jean was a submissive who loved to relinquish control and yield to Pandora's desires. He enjoyed being led in the bedroom. He became her obedient pet.

The next night she was on top of him straddling him. She rode him so fast, so hard, so aggressively. He'd never felt more humiliated. Her large breasts were bouncing up and down on his face and he was moaning in despair. He was getting close to his climax; he was breathing hard and grunting quietly and then she heard:

"*Please! Please, I can't!*"

"*Please stop! I cannot, I feel like I am going to pass out! I feel like I am going to faint.*" He whimpered as he ejaculated twice. She stopped and kissed him on the forehead, giving him a cold glass of water. He needed rest as tomorrow their medieval adventure began!

The Cathars were a religious 12th-century group who emerged in the Languedoc region of France, shrouded in mystery. They pursued the teachings of the lost hidden knowledge. They invoked the secret knowledge through initiation rituals and alchemy, much of which was lost. The Cathars were hunted down and burnt alive along with their many secrets.
The Cathar castle was majestic perched atop a cliff, overlooking a breathtaking valley below. Surrounded by grassy valleys and reminiscent of a fairy tale setting yet its history was more macabre. Pandora searched for the ghost of Dame Blanche in the Puilaurens fortress north tower- known as Puilaurens' White Lady. Legend has it, that she stopped at the castle in 1353, while she was on her way to Spain, she was locked up in the tower at the age of twenty-two and since then her ghost haunts the castle towers.

They drove to Rennes-le-Château Church to see the ancient church which harboured a sinister secret. Just around its entrance corner - a menacing devil statue, also known as Asmodeus, crouching in the shadows. For centuries, the statue struck fear into the hearts of visitors and locals alike. This sleepy village held within its walls a trove of enigmatic tales, with a history that stretched back to times pre-dating the advent of Christianity.

As Pandora immersed herself in the history of the village and poured over its ancient manuscripts, she uncovered a remarkable link between her lost love Frederic's ancestor, and a haunting love story that had unfolded in the village centuries ago. Deep within the heart of the medieval village, a forbidden romance had blossomed between a female vampire and a human farmer, ultimately culminating in tragedy. This ill-fated love affair left behind a legacy of sorrow and unresolved destiny. Within the ancient manuscript, she found the poignant words:

"His love was veiled in darkness, profound and unspoken. He loved her in secret."

Jean drove her into town for a much-needed dinner and wine. He ordered her a delightful Caprice des Anges wine, a rose from the Languedoc region. Upon seeing the name of the wine, she was overcome with melancholy, and the sight of her ex's name in red graffiti on the nearby wall only deepened her emotions - Frederic! Sitting beneath the parasol of a quaint bistro, a gentle breeze brushed her cheek as if carrying a whisper of Frederic's presence. A bitter-sweet smile crossed her face as she felt his lingering spirit throughout the trip. Memories of their time together flooded her, and she felt as though he was finally sending her the long-awaited sign that he was with her. The name, Caprice des Anges, reminded her of the nickname he had given her mood swings. Coincidence is magic in action!

As their journey drew to a close, Jean drove her to the train station. Just before parting, he sealed their farewell with a passionate kiss and left her with a small, delicate ceramic frog as a parting gift!

DATING

Pandora was simply running in circles with nothing appealing to taste. However, there was some hope in her black heart. Despite the odds, she believed that true love had the power to find her and break her curse. In the meantime, she found solace in her own arms. She waited for the next Wolf Moon to meet the vampire witch spirits. As the moon radiated with reflective energy, smoke seeped in through the corner of her room, and one by one they emerged and whispered their blessings and consolations to her. Renewed and energized by their words, she started looking for her new date. Could he be her beloved?

Late into the night, she dedicated herself to meticulously swiping through a myriad of profiles on a dating app. The incoming flood of messages from potential matches was both exciting and abhorrent.

"I spent most of the year abroad so my energy is a bit depleted. You know New York? I have nothing planned apart from a wedding in Sweden. But I have other tentative plans for summer. So.. tell me about your career plans... what are your ambitions ..where do you like to shop..."

"I lifted my legs on Friday, pumped my arms on Saturday, and my upper body today. Now I got a massage. My joints ache. Come massage me. "

"Shut up! Get out of the house or I will come and carry you out! "

MISTER HOLLYWOOD

ALFONSO

In front of the bar door stood a little man called Alfonso a man she met on-line, who looked as if he had been made of the same material as the barstools and was about a meter fifty centimetres high at most. He was a very short man resembling a snarly small dog with deep brown eyes. His posture was erect, and his chest puffed out like a gorilla, in an attempt to make himself seem bigger. She wasn't happy when she saw him, she could tell this date would be a bore and she needed a stiff drink. It was a typical generic bar with bland outdated furniture and artwork hung on the walls to appeal to the shallow masses with little or no personality. The menu consisted of fish and chips, chips and more chips along with the drink menu.

As they entered the bar, they exchanged warm greetings. She flashed a sincere smile and politely asked if he could fetch her a whiskey. There was an air of self-assuredness as she strolled over to the opposite side of the bar, choosing to settle into the embrace of a luxurious yellow velvet sofa instead of perching atop a lofty wrought iron chair, all to ensure they were on the same eye level. She was keenly aware of not wanting to come across as intimidating to him, knowing all too well that it might pique his interest. She could tell he loved a dominatrix! She was determined to make a good impression as she was a bit of a bitch on her previous date. A single headshot and a brief phone conversation were all they had shared thus far; she hadn't had the opportunity to really get to know him. Perhaps the driving force to meet him, wasn't so much her interest in him, but rather to be out of the apartment.

As he placed the order for her drink, she found a glimmer of hope in the gesture, appreciating the promise of a strong drink and perhaps even reconsidering her initial impression of him. Walking past him, she made a detour to the bathroom, to touch up her lipstick.

Alfonso looked at her and gave her a flirty smile and said: *"Nice Boobs!"*

As he ordered a double whiskey for Pandora and a cup of black coffee for himself, he stood at the bar, his head reaching only to the top of the counter.

"Bloody hell! That's a stiff drink you ordered! I don't drink. I do martial arts!" He snarled.

He had the muscles but not the look that most people would describe as "Hollywood good-looking". He was the epitome of everything she found insufferable, and it was shaping up to be a dreadfully boring evening.

The conversation suddenly steered to her favourite topic -the supernatural!

"So, what do you do for fun?" he asked with a smirk.

Pandora's eyes sparkled mischievously as she toyed with her whisky glass, her fangs itching to come out. *"Oh, you know, the usual,"* she replied casually. *"I dabble in a bit of magic, indulge in the occasional spellbinding..."*

Alfonso laughed dismissively. *"Magic, huh? Sounds like you've been watching too many fantasy movies,"* he said, taking a sip of his coffee.

Pandora's red lips curved into a dangerous smile. *"Believe me, darling, my magic is very real."*

"Sure, it is, sweetheart," he said, oblivious to the danger he was in. *"Don't tell me you are one of those spirit-chasing crazies. Do you believe in fairies and unicorns as well?"*. He barked at her in his pompous fake English accent.

"Crazy is not the word I would use," she replied calmly. *"I've seen things you couldn't even begin to imagine."*

He sat back looking at her with his arms crossed. *"Oh Yeah? like what?"*

She told him a tale of the night she was attacked in her bed by a gang of smoke spirits who tried to possess her body.

"That is the most far-fetched story I have ever heard," he laughed. *"I don't know if you are playing me for a fool or if you are actually a kook."*

"It happened."

"You don't know what you are talking about. You just made this whole thing up," he said mockingly.

"Don't be so quick to dismiss my words," she warned.

"*Oh really?*"

She looked around her and spied the young waitress with a tray of drinks. She was in desperate need of another. As the evening dragged on, Pandora sipped her drink thoughtfully, trying not to lose all her expensive lipstick on this cheap date. Her eyes wandered over other men in the bar who seemed more interesting. She was dressed simple yet sexy in a black lace top. Her posture was relaxed, but alert, in case she needed to run out. Her date Alfonso had as much mystery as a blocked toilet had to a plumber.

Alfonso with a smirk playing on his lips, leaned closer to her, his voice dropping to a low intimate tone.

"*You know Pandora*", he began, swirling his cold cup of coffee. "*I am an actor. I have just finished filming in Iceland.*"

As they sat across from each other in a dimly lit bar, he prattled on about his auditions, barely taking a breath between boasts. Pandora rolled her eyes discreetly, her mind wandering to more interesting topics, like the taste of blood and the power of magic. He was used to getting what he wanted and tonight he wanted sex. In truth, he was a B movie horror actor who no one ever heard of.

Pandora smiled politely but didn't miss the underlying presumptions in his tone.

"*It was nice meeting you!*" She said abruptly feeling that she was wasting her time and his.

"*It could get even nicer you know*", he said, his desperate brown puppy eyes peering hard into her soul.

"*My car is parked just around the corner. Why don't we take this somewhere more private eh? My place is not far from here or we can just make out in my car.*"

Pandora raised an eyebrow, her tight smile remaining but with a hint of darkness creeping into her voice.

"*Are you inviting me for sex on a first date?*"

"*We both know where this is heading, don't we? I can sense some strong sexual tension between us. Why waste time.*" He said, his tone both confident and patronizing.

Pandora put down her glass, her eyes filled with blood locking with his unwaveringly.

"*True, but sometimes one must be careful of what he wants!*"

Alfonso's impatience began to show.

"*C'mon, let's get in my car. We can play inside. Oh, my film is coming out next month. I can tell you all the gossip.*"

Pandora met his gaze in a composed deadly stare.

"*I came here to inspect you and enjoy my drink. Perhaps you should go back to shagging peasants.*"

He masked his irritation with a forced smile his rotten teeth gleaming at her. Each tooth was stained with years of decay and neglect, for someone who didn't drink and smoke it was very odd.

"*Well, you are full of surprises. We will be in touch*", he said rising from his seat.

Pandora walked away from this date with her head held high and with burning anger. She knew that night she was going to curse him. She knew that if she left and joined him in his car he could make her a semi-famous actress in his horror B movies, but she wanted a small amount of revenge against him. A pang of guilt hit her, but not hard enough to deter her from what she wanted to do. She knew how to use her powers well, and if she put her mind to it, she knew she could curse him in a smart way. Mr Hollywood was on his way to stardom!

Once at home, she took a deep breath and silently cursed him with his fame. With the utterance of her final word, Alfonso felt as if the entire universe had come to a standstill. His movements ceased, his breath held, and even his thoughts halted. He could only ponder if he was in the midst of an out-of-body experience or caught in a surreal trance. Gradually, he found himself in a realm where the stars shone with an unparalleled brilliance he never seen before. Gaging his surroundings, he realized that he was no longer on Earth.

"*Welcome to Hollywood!*" a resounding voice declared.

"*Bloody Hell! W-what? Who are you?*" he asked. He saw a large figure, but also a small one in the distance. The more he stared, the bigger it got until it reached an indescribable size. His eyes burned from the starlight, and he couldn't look away, yet still he stared.

"*Do you really want to know who I am, or would you rather call me a spirit chasing crazy!*" Pandora giggled.

THE ITALIAN STALLION

CASTRO

He resembled the sadistic Bluebeard in a metaphorical sense. The story goes as such; Bluebeard who was a wealthy man and a murderous husband who soon after marriage had gone away on a long business trip leaving his new wife with the keys. The keys were to all doors within the castle, except for one door, which he forbade her to open. The new wife disobeyed the husband and out of curiosity opened the forbidden door, discovering the bodies of his former wives. In life sometimes such doors need to be closed forever never to be explored. Such as Pandora's relationship with Castro.

He was of Italian origin residing in London and Liverpool, a successful businessman and a hobby photographer. He was in his late forties with a long beard and long brown hair, with wicked eyebrows, resembling a wicked monk.

She had been involved with him on and off for two years, meeting him in the world of online dating. He appealed to her by his intellect and masculinity, and when she first locked eyes with him, she felt a surge of electricity through her body and electrifying sexual chemistry.

Their first date lasted six hours, they talked about ghosts, science, and current affairs of the modern world. She felt that this man could stimulate both her mind and her body!

"I do not like the word Master, but we should find a safe word. I like to slap the face, the body, and I like to inflict pain," he told her on their first meeting.

"You know many call me the Italian Stallion," he said with a glint in his eyes, fishing for praise.

This Italian Stallion was fond of organic wines and whips, but with his saggy ass and wrinkled balls, was he really The Stallion folk of Liverpool talked of. There were rumours of a tall sadistic foreigner fucking all the women. Pandora wondered to herself if he was worth the risk, but by some magic, she was drawn to him.

He carried himself with an air of superiority and dramatic gestures. He had a commanding tone that brooked no arguments. He exuded belief in his superiority and loved control. He loved to control in the bedroom, taking the lead, guiding, and directing her body. He took immense pleasure in inflicting pain on her with each smack and slap. He loved seeing her in distress and feeling a sense of power over her physically and emotionally. She gritted her teeth as he whipped her hard and greedily with a bamboo stick. After ejaculating, he would fall into the bed exasperated and soon after falling asleep. Snoring loudly into dawn.

Their affair continued for two years, where they would meet at The Hotel of One Hundred

Faces. He always booked the most lavish of the rooms. Rich crimson hues dominated the chamber, shrouding it in an opulent diabolical ambiance. The walls were adorned with intricate wallpaper of weeping cherubs in shades of gold and black. Dim soft lighting cast a warm glow on his olive skin and a creepy emerging smile on his face. There stood an elaborate carved antique bed, draped in layers of satin and velvet. A large crystal chandelier hung from the ceiling; shimmering reflections from the crystals across her naked body as if fire fairies were dancing! The air of the room was perfumed with his heavy cologne of spice and incense. On the bed lay a black leather flogger crafted from the finest Italian leather, highest-quality suede, and his initials embossed in gold on the handle. The flogger was perfect for teasing her sensitive pale skin with its soft trailing suede fronds, taking full swings on her ass, breasts and building up to the red marks on her skin. The night invited her to indulge her senses in a decadent retreat of lavish indulgence with a little bit of pain and pleasure.

He lay idly on the bed and yawned, *"No resolution for the New Year coming, apart from spanking and fucking!"*

"You know I am also known as Il Vampiro de Londres," he winked, unzipping his tight pants.

She was on her knees now ready to suck him off. He was watching her intently. He watched her lick his cock a few more times before she slid her tongue along the shaft to his balls. He moaned intensely while watching. She pulled his cock between her lips and took him as much as she could. Her fingers teased his saggy balls a bit, and her other hand slid up his body to pinch his fragile nipple.

"You make me feel like I am... I am on ... drugs," he breathed sporadically, trying to catch his breath.

He would whip her until she was red and raw. She was never permitted to complain. It was always a question of what she deserved. And the redder she was, the more pleased he was with her.

Pandora was not really a submissive, but over the centuries her heart became so numb and cold, that she needed to feel the flames of a horsewhip to bring her back to life and resuscitate her from her waking dream. He told her often, that he wanted to slap her with the greatest force possible, staring at her with his dark profound eyes burning with depravity. His features would become hollow and after sex, he looked much older than he was.

Another night after taking him deeper than before, she felt some kind of love had grown. Before ejaculating, he cried out so loudly in the room, shaking the walls and scaring the other guests in the hotel.

"Ti Amo!"

As time went by, he became increasingly affectionate towards her in bed, gratifying her with loving caresses and passionate long kisses. He held her tightly in bed until they would both dose off to sleep, clutching each other's hands. When the morning came, he was still erect and wanted more of her. She was hopeful that one night he would tell her she was his one and only, but he did not, instead he would say to her:

"You be surprised how many really young girls love an old man!" He scoffed in his theatrical Italian accent. *"And I don't even need to try!"* He laughed. She understood that the nicer and more loving she was to him, the crueller he became.

One night in bed, she mentioned that she would be too busy to see him that week. Her dear friend Ambrose was coming into town.

"A man?! A lover!!" He growled.

"Well, yes. As we are not official, I have a few lovers. Didn't you know?" She smiled at him. She was lying. There was no one, there was only him.

Without words, he lashed out and slapped her arm, leaving a large red handprint, and forced her head to suck him. She cried out at the pain and tried to pull back, but his hand held her there, her face buried in his crotch. She felt her heart race in fear, she was so terrified! It was a passionate smack, which showed her a glimpse of his jealousy, abusive nature, and his double standards. The spell has been broken, her superhuman senses have returned to her and she could read him like a book now. He was toxic.

She was exploring what this world had to offer in terms of love. She has played with fire before and never got burnt, but this time this creep was starting to crawl under her skin. His soul was poison, and she chose to hate him. That night she contacted Dwarf Melmoth to trace further into Castro's past life and find out who he really was.

In the Castle of Depravo, nestled on the waters of Venice, there resided the Count Cogliostro, he was feared by both men and women. He was a man of power; and wealth and he was a sexual deviant. Pandora knew she recognized him from somewhere. In his former life, he was known as the famous and self-styled magician Count Cogliostro, who fucked his victims in the throat, both men and women. But he preferred the young flesh of women the most. The younger they were, the easier they were to mould to his will, like play dough! Within the stone walls of his castle, he would test the boundaries of their submission. His life was a dark symphony of passion and pain. He was known for his uncontrollable sexual appetite and as he was an eccentric figure associated with the Royal Courts of Venice, he remained untouchable. As his past relationships deepened with his subjects, the passion turned to pain and romance into pure sadism. He began to frighten them. Beneath his façade of sophistication lurked a primal savage. No one could satisfy his insatiable hunger for submission. One night in their darkest moment, his young lovers gathered and drowned him in the Venice canal. Cogliostro's past life of glamour was behind him, and he was reborn into a mere mortal called Castro with little recollection of who he once was. Even though Castro had no recollection of his past life, the traits of Count Cogliostro remained.

After confirming her suspicions about him, a haunting feeling weighed heavily on her heart, where her every romantic endeavour seemed in vain and thwarted by unseen forces, destined for failure. She felt trapped in a circle of disappointments, despite her best efforts to find her Beloved! She decided to end her affair with Castro.

When the long affair ended, he continued to contact her and request to see her.

"You want to be punished!"

"You want to be spanked!"

"I am free on Monday."

It was always Monday or Thursday, never the weekend for their meetings, as on the weekend he would be in bed with many others.

She ignored his messages as in her eyes he was just a pitiful old fool whom she did not respect, and he had served his purpose. There was a time when she felt great love for him, but from his side, it was purely lust and mockery. She laughed deep into the night at how pathetic he was and felt great sadness for his many victims. No heart deserved so much confusion and pain! That night, on the Waning Moon, she devised a perfect punishment for him!

The ingredients for her spell were in her truth and her intention, for the potion ingredients, held no magic in their structure. It was all in the intention and belief. The magic words came easily.

Out of enchanted black swamp wax, she made a full body image of Castro and a full image of a monstrous hound. She placed these items on her altar at opposite ends. In her cauldron a lock of his hair, his belt which he gifted her, and a tooth of a wild hound from the netherworld. She turned and kneeled before the cauldron, picking up the evergreen twigs from the Forest of Confusion. Setting fire to each twig from the cauldron candle, she blew them out with her intent and put them inside the cauldron.

She exclaimed:

"Full Moon desire , My heart is on Fire!
"Thus we banish him into the darkest winter night, from the human form.

"We welcome JUSTICE in our plight!

Say farewell to what is dead, his heart and his morbid soul, and go into the night as an ugly Hound!

And let us greet each living thing,

We welcome new beginnings! "

As she recited this seven times, she drew the wax objects closer together until they were face to face. After the incantation, she threw the wax figures into the cauldron and let the fire do its magic.

"Now you are a dog. Go! Wherever you please!"

Castro was transformed into a dog who was weathered by years of hunting its prey, his coat was black with patches of grey. Massive pendulous testicles hung between his legs which were oversized for his frame. They swayed each step he took, drawing curious glances and laughter from people. His teeth sharpened into fangs and his eyes turned haunting ochre.

The roles have been switched; she was his master now. As an old hound, he would not leave her alone, his tail wagging, he dogged her wherever she went and never left her side. As a human, he was used to sleeping with her one night a week, and the next night with his regulars, and the third night with his 4th and 5th. But now, he only slept outside her door. Bored and suffocated by him, she banished him to roam the Forest of Confusion for all eternity.

In the Forest of Confusion was The Castle of Virgins, standing at a foothill isolated from anything else living. The hound roamed aimlessly in the forest, sniffing, and looking for his next young victims. After days of roaming ceaselessly, he came across The Castle of Virgins.

The castle stood protected by a tall, spiked fence surrounded by ghostly mist. Towering walls and turrets weathered by eras past, but within the ancient walls behind a large window a lively playful scene unfolded.

A large window overlooked the sprawling black forest below. Through its heavy panes, angelic golden rays cast a warm pinkish glow, illuminating the room within. Inside the room, a group of young women gathered, their gentle laughter echoing off the stone murals. They were dressed in pink flowing gowns, with long hair like honey silk framing their smiling faces, as they chatted and giggled. Among them was Amelia, with her sparkling eyes and infectious laugh, and Greta, with her freckles and dimpled cheeks. They were joined by Annabelle, whose melodious pure voice filled the room with more laughter. Their laughter and voices rose and fell like the gentle swell of an ocean.

Encircling the castle was a formidable barrier, a giant spiked fence crafted from black iron. The fence stretched far and wide forming a protective ring around the castle. The towering fence loomed over anyone who dared to pass by, but the imposing fence did not dissuade the eager hound. Its eyes locked on the window, and with saliva dripping from its jaws, it leapt at the tempting sight, attempting to clear the fence. However, the ambitious jump ended in a painful grotesque failure, as the fence mangled the hound's balls, leaving it trapped within the confines of the castle. His destiny was set, he was an old hound without his balls and trapped forever in the forest inside the grounds of The Castle of Virgins, unable to escape temptation and unable to feed his perversions. It was a gruesome spell so rightfully forged especially for him from fire to the moon!

It was difficult for Pandora to control her contempt for humanity as it grew fiercer after each disappointing encounter and the realisation that the human world was made up mostly of fools and rogues. It became clear to her that she could not entertain the hope of finding in someone the same love and loyalty. She was already dreaming of retiring to her life of refined solitude in the magical forest, seeking refuge in its magic from the unending deluge of mortal depravity. For her, this world was a confusing mess of love and emotional indifference, and profound suffering.

ANDOR MOON

Pandora had been in a casual relationship with Andor Moon for seven months. Andor was an imposing, dominant figure with the physique of a well-seasoned bodybuilder. His sculpted biceps seemed like massive boulders, a result of countless hours of intense training. His muscular body could captivate any woman. On the surface, he was the envy of most men and what you would call a fuck boy. Yet despite his imposing sexual presence his mind remained unblessed by intellect and his eyes were dead, much to Pandora's bemusement.

He could never satisfy the darkness in her. He was her simple sex beast in the forest who whispered:

"I am your desire; I will set you free. You love me".

Despite his lack of intellect, he was a master of seduction and pleasure. He artfully weaved his way through the opulent and exclusive circles of high society, captivating a discerning crowd of wealthy, mature women who savoured the finest dining experiences at Michelin-starred establishments and indulged in the exquisite collection of Hermes handbags as a leisurely pursuit. However, concealed beneath his seemingly vacant stare, lay a deeply sentimental and nostalgic heart, yearning for a genuine connection with another. Pandora kept him around for her sexual gratification. Afterall he could ejaculate 7 times per night! Pandora, with her keen perception, was able to see past Andor's carefully constructed facade and discern the emptiness that lay hidden behind his lifeless, blue eyes.

"You love me. Say it! I know you do," was the recurring plea that he often directed towards her, a phrase that held a strange place in their complex relationship.

A poem of Emily Dickinson echoed in her mind as she imagined her life with him:

"I cannot live with You –

It would be Life –

And Life is over there –

Behind the Shelf"

He wanted to possess her. He wanted her to love him. And once she would give in, he would abandon her. Eventually, she would become the discarded boring housewife. To watch her suffer was his serenity and joy, but his greatest satisfaction lay in her submission to him.

Andor was born into a proud Hungarian family with a rich gypsy heritage and eventually found himself working as a private chauffeur in the bustling city of London. Unbeknownst to him, his family history held a remarkable secret—a lineage that could be traced back to a noble clan of werewolves who had long served as protectors of the Carpathian Forest witches and the Forbidden Forest of the netherworld. This hidden legacy came to light when Pandora caught sight of a striking amulet that Andor always wore around his neck: a meticulously crafted wolf fang made of bloodstone with a red engraving *"Servant of the Moon"*. It was a cherished gift from his great uncle Attila on his 16th birthday.

As the nights deepened, Andor found himself plagued by vivid and unsettling dreams that seemed to magnify with each full moon. Nightmares of primal hunger and a wildness that seemed to grip his soul.

He was unaware of his supernatural heritage and dismissed his dreams as figments of an overactive imagination. His days were spent honing his physique and evenings charming the rich women of Mayfair. Yet as the days turned into weeks and the weeks into months, Pandora could no longer deny him his truth and as fate would have it, his destiny was about to be revealed.

On the crag of the pink full moon, the city was immersed in a surreal, ethereal silver light, casting an unearthly glow upon the urban landscape. The air hung heavy and still, shattered only by the eerie symphony of rats scurrying and cockroaches skittering through the labyrinthine alleys of the forsaken city. It was in this haunting ambiance that Pandora, feeling the pull of his ancient lineage, called upon the mystical energies of his werewolf clan, seeking to rouse the dormant essence of his lycanthropic ancestry. On that dark night feeling playful, she invited Andor to her flat. Without words spoken he untied her red lace chemise and undressed himself, exposing his giant hairy chest and well-endowed penis. She looked at his naked body, his broad chest and the muscles on his arms and legs, his manhood rising up with excitement. She could see the desire in his eyes. She turned her back; he was now standing behind her and she felt his hardness against her ass.

"You love me, Pandora."

She smiled weakly and replied, *"Hmm... Yes I do."*

"Come, my love, I have a new game for you," Pandora said while stroking Andor's huge

cock.

"*A new game? What is it?*" he asked as his eyes lit up.

"*It's called 'Survival'.*" Pandora smiled.

"*What are the rules?*"

"*I will send your mind into the realm of nightmares, and you must survive and find a way to escape. You'll have to fight, and use your primal instincts, and your strength. If you can survive in there, I'll give you the best reward of your life.*"

"*And if I lose?*"

"*If you die, then I'll just keep fucking your corpse.*" Pandora giggled as she licked her blood-red lips and her eyes glowed purple.

She was naked, her large breasts, which hung down in their own heaviness, were tipped with pink, pointy hard nipples, and her long slender legs, though muscular, still held their soft womanliness. The sight of her body sent an overwhelming surge through him, and he took her by the waist and lifted her to his mouth so that he could suckle those huge, soft, round breasts. Her body was now wet from his tongue as it slid in long languid strokes down the length of her abdomen and into the softness between her thighs. His penis was rigid and throbbing with life as she knelt down before him. Her long black hair framed her beautiful oval face. She was looking up at him as her lips encircled the tip of his shaft. He was mesmerized by the sight of his large thick cock disappearing between her red lips and into the deep warmth of her mouth. Her hand slid slowly up and down the length of him while she sucked the tip and rolled her tongue around the rim.

"*Mmm...you taste so...sweet...*" she smiled.

Something stirred within him, he was more aggressive than usual, his kisses were bites, leaving visible purple marks on her porcelain neck and arms. It was almost as if he was marking his territory. His hands were all over her body. Pandora felt him swell and explode inside her, his seed coating her inner walls. He pulled out and she felt him run down her leg.

"*More!*" she begged.

"*Anything for you.*"

"*Fuck my ass, I want to feel you one last time.*"

"*Ok,*" he said, grabbing her ass and spreading her cheeks.

She felt him push against her tight opening, the tip of his cock entering her. It hurt, but it was a good pain, the kind of pain she liked. The kind of pain that made her feel alive.

She let out a groan, her heart was beating fast, she felt her cheeks turn bright red, and she felt something flow inside her. As he was starting to bite harder on her neck, a loud knock on the door disturbed them, it was the spirit of Attila his werewolf uncle.

"*It is time.*" The spell has begun.

Suddenly a searing pain tore through Andors' body, his skin rippled, his bones elongated and fur began sprouting from his pores. Andor began to growl unleashing his suppressed primal power! He tried to speak but his voice broke into ugly howls. He became possessed by bloodlust! Pandora wondered if his rich ladies would become his suddenly slaughtered cattle. Brittles formed under his tongue, yet his dead eyes remained human. He stumbled and fell to his knees, his anguished howls blending with the dissonant chorus of the nocturnal world. Every muscle and bone in his body contorted and shifted as he experienced the terrifying metamorphosis into a savage and powerful werewolf! Andor's eyes widened in disbelief as Pandora pronounced his fate, condemning him to the eerie depths of The Forbidden Forest, where he was to serve as the guardian of the ancient witch clans.

"*Your first mistake was thinking that I am one of your sheep!*" Growled Andor, before disappearing into the darkness.

WEREWOLF
ANDOR

THE WITCH HUNTERS

CHAD

It was like any other week; winter sunlight was filtering gently through the white lace curtains of her bedroom window. It was another tedious week planned with new encounters and dates, but there was a profound stillness and the smell of death; a faint sound of "Meow" was heard from the corner of her bedroom. It was Bones, her beloved cat, who had been with her for eternity. There he lay, lifeless. He was of esteemed age, even older than most witch cats. His once sleek fur was now a patchwork of greys and blacks, and his whiskers were long and drooping to the floor. His vibrant primal yellow eyes were now cloudy and covered with a veil of death. Pandora and Bones had been through so much together. He was her trusted confidant and a constant presence in her life - her first real love. On her date nights, he would climb into her wardrobe and carefully select the perfect outfit for her by pawing at the chosen clothes. He had a knack for knowing which fragrances suited her best, guiding her with gentle taps on the selected items. And when she was tired, he would give her a massage, kneading softly and deliberately at her back and head.

There he was lifeless! It felt as if her heart had been ripped open leaving a gaping wound that no one would fill. The last time she felt this way was when she lost her greatest love, Frederic. Unfortunately, no magic could bring him back, as Bone's time in the human realm has come to an end. The memory of his final moments lingered vividly in her mind; she could still feel the warmth of his fur and see the sadness and confusion in his eyes as he glanced at her. Throughout that entire week, her apartment felt haunted by his presence. His loving energy seemed to permeate every room, leaving behind fleeting glimpses of his shadow. Whenever she saw her Scottish wool throw on the sofa, she could not help but be reminded of him. It was the same spot where he used to stretch out and bask in the sunlight, and she half-expected him to appear at any moment, greeting her as he always did. But instead, there was only the deafening silence.

That particular weekend, she found herself anticipating a prearranged meet-up with a captivating and mysterious man she had encountered on a dating app. His name was Chad Rorschach. Their communication had spanned three weeks of texting, and the much-anticipated meet-up was set for that Saturday. However, grief held her in its powerful and unpredictable grip. It surged through her like waves, at times overwhelming her like a relentless tsunami. Anticipation for the date was overshadowed by moments of profound sorrow and guilt, leaving her with little excitement. Despite the upcoming meeting, she still found solace in conversations with Bones, seeking to comfort his spirit and offering apologies for not being able to prevent his passing. Although well-meaning acquaintances attempted to console her by dismissing Bones as "just a cat," their words felt hollow. They could not comprehend the profound depth of love and loyalty that Pandora felt for him.

The day of her date arrived, her hands trembled as she applied the blackest mascara on her puffy eyelids, as tears streaked down her face. Her once aquamarine eyes were now puffy and red from days of weeping for her beloved cat. She glanced nonchalantly at her closet and chose black- she did not put any effort into her outfit. Everything seemed so meaningless. She dowsed herself in her favourite perfume of Bulgarian Rose and Geranium from a secluded gothic garden where the allure of bloody roses proved to be irresistible. This perfume made her feel like the happiest vampire deeply in love with another vampire embracing in darkness eternal yearning for his love. It was perfect!

She was running late, and with a sense of dread mingling with sorrow, she put on a brave face. Chad, a strikingly handsome and athletic man of Mâori descent, shared a similar lineage with Kanuweia, her closest and dearest friend. His unexpected invitation for a date caught her off guard, given her perception that men like him, who epitomized the "jock" type, rarely showed interest in witches like her. They were too superficial for her and incompatible with her values, and she viewed herself as too weird for them. Her suspicions intensified, and she could not shake the feeling that there might be an ulterior motive behind his interest in her. It was evident that he was captivated by her practice of witchcraft and her mind, leaving her questioning the sincerity of his intentions. This witchcraft was something she regretted mentioning to him as she was judged many times for her interests in the occult, but this was who she was, and she was not going to live under people's scriptures forever. Over three weeks of chatting with him, she was inundated with tests, quizzes, and questions about her character and her private life. She did not mind as she wanted to understand herself better and she was aware he may have used her as a subject for one of his custom-tailored databases he was designing for work, after all, he was a Psychometrician. However, he seemed open to her darkness, and she was curious to explore the darkness in him.

She met him at one of her favourite sushi restaurants called Yôkai. As she descended the stairs to the dining area, he caught sight of her from his table, and she could sense his disappointment. His expression lacked any trace of a smile. Being a vampire, she could discern his thoughts. He had expected her to be flawless and well put-together, with a designer handbag, impeccably dressed, and sporting a Brazilian blowout. Instead, Pandora seemed to have lost her otherworldly radiance, wearing a worn winter sweater over old jeggings, her hair dishevelled, and mascara streaking down her face.

"So, tell me about your witchcraft", he said impatiently. His presence was imposing with a muscular physique, but never for a minute, his physique intimidated her, after all, it was just

flesh and flesh was not forever. His eyes were truly what could unsettle people. They were deep and flowing with the intensity of undefined colours. They were not just looking at her, they were looking through her, into the darkest recesses of her mind.

They conveyed a sense of deadly focus like hellfire. She could tell that simple folk would be unnerved by his eyes and captured by their overbearing stare, but Pandora had already seen the depths of hell. His eyes were familiar to her. A demon lurked in them, and she was no stranger to them. They were pesky little creatures!

"*My ancestors were witch hunters,*" he said. She pretended not to pay attention, but his words struck her.

She was not hungry, she just wanted to get drunk, to drown in her grief. She ate half of her salmon nigiri before she excused herself to the bathroom to cry. When she came back, Chad had a worried look on his face.

"*Oh no, I hope you are okay, I am really interested to know more about the witchcraft.*"

"*I feel like going to a bar and just getting a little drunk. I'm feeling a bit down about my cat.*" She struggled to hold back tears, her voice barely above a whisper.

"*I'm so sorry. Sounds like a plan.*" He said sincerely, getting his coat.

They went out of the restaurant to a bar across the street. She so desperately wanted to cry into his arms and for him to console her and tell her it was ok, but he remained cold and clinical. He was there only for one purpose, and it was not romantic. He examined her minutely; she was surprised that her skin did not walk off her body.

Throughout the evening her intuition was correct, there was something more to him, a darkness that wanted answers to her secrets. His ancestors were witch hunters! This demonic hunter had a worthy opponent a vampire witch! A thousand years ago, these hunters were willing to risk their lives to protect their land against magic. The demonic witch hunters ravaged the witch clans, imprisoning them in crude cages and plundering their ancient knowledge and resources. In response, a clandestine Order of the Serpent emerged, comprising extraordinary individuals trained to elude the hunters by traversing alternate dimensions. Among their ranks was Pandora's ancestor, her uncle Wilmot. The sinister witch hunters transmitted their ability to detect witches through the generations, culminating in the emergence of Chad. Deep beneath the surface from the watch of docile humans, a secret invisible magic war was fought.

Chad had a sharp intellect and was interested in delving into the mysteries of the human psyche seeking to understand others and himself, but he was not alone. A demon had attached itself to him, its evil presence lurking in the shadows of his soul. Despite Chad's scientific mind, his understanding of human emotions remained shallow. His fascination with the human psyche was purely academic, devoid of empathy or genuine connection with the soul of a person. In truth, he was looking for a rich hot woman, who would be accepted by his peers and who would elevate his status in modern society, a society based on luxury and tedious dinner parties filled with forgotten aristocrats. The "royal courts" are full of bored and useless people, but they are also the most powerful. These dinner parties contain some of the most powerful people in the kingdom, who are talking about the most boring topics you can imagine whilst flashing their diamonds.

"I hear there's a new rich Countess in town!" She said coyly.

"But you know..."

"But what?" He asked with a puzzled look on his face.

"She doesn't seem to be quite Normal." She said drunkenly. She giggled at the thought that he did not know who he was dealing with.

He observed people as mere specimens to be studied, their emotions were data points to be analysed and graphs to plot. She could tell that he was driven by a relentless force to prove himself worthy to his peers and he was on a journey of self-discovery. He wanted to understand who he was, and he wanted to understand the demon in him. He was not aware himself of how far he delved into the ancient forbidden knowledge and what dark entities attached themselves to him. This man was torn between the obligation to his witch-hunter ancestors and to live a modern human life full of frivolous riches. In his quest for power and status, he risked losing himself to the very dark forces he sought to command.

The evening went well, Chad was calm and composed, he provided her the quiet strength she needed, and he was like a giant sequoia tree. This was the first date on which she felt weak. Her emotions were all over the place. He was the perfect and most generous drinking companion plying her with her favourite expensive rose wine, glass after glass. He was the ideal "therapist" she so needed that night! After ten glasses of wine, Pandora felt inebriated and when the bar closing hour came, he walked her home.

After arriving at her apartment Pandora was happy to be alone and she was glad for not revealing the secrets of her magic, even under the influence of alcohol. Except she was not alone! A wintry wandering wind swept across her bedroom and there was an inexplicable awareness that she was not alone, she had a feeling of being observed by unseen entities from beyond the veil of the living. Another chaotic wind entered through her second window, and she felt one hundred eyes upon her, not even her amulets could prevent them from entering her flat. It was an eerie unsettling sensation that sent a shiver down her neck and her heart racing with dread. With the wind came the doors that banged and with the doors came the musky smell of graves, and with it came the long hands. The wind announced to her the arrival of new unwelcomed guests-the witch hunters!

She went to bed trying to ignore the sensation and to stay protected in her sacred circle, but she felt bony long hands pulling down her covers, hands on her body twisting and turning her like a ragdoll.

"Fuck Off!" She screamed.

"I am not interested! You are boring me."

She quickly sprayed the room with her Aura spray she concocted a week prior, infused with Amethyst crystals from the caves of the Dwarves Kingdom, Labradorite stones from the depth of magma, Angelika root, and Juniper berries gifted by her dear friend Kanuweia. One demon still lingered - Gaap, Chad's personal demon. This powerful entity resonated at a lower frequency, as it was none other than the Prince of Hell. Legend has it that at noon, Gaap could take on human form, stirring up intense feelings of both love and hatred, and could transport the possessed to other realms, even invading their dreams. The demon would mock and torment its victims in a long-forgotten language like Akkadian, evoking powerful and overwhelming emotions. For humans are all fallen angels, their emotions and imaginations can often be in error. They desire the things they should not, shun the things they should value, and are emotionally attached to things that work to their destruction. Demons know these weaknesses and manipulate them through diabolical temptations! Tonight, it was cloaked in the guise of the darkness of the night with smouldering red eyes and black wings that cast sinister long shadows on her walls.

Though his presence is unnoticed by mortal eyes, a witch or a vampire would easily recognize it. Pandora was too sad and tired of his tricks; she was not going to play- she just laughed at it. She did not fear darkness for darkness was her light! The demon was intrigued by her magic and seduced by her sorrow, he wanted to test her. Demons love to attach themselves to sorrow, and they love to play tricks! Frustrated by her resilience and bored with her apathy, he left never to return. She would never see the demon again and nor would she ever meet Chad again. It was a reminder of how very little separated her and the human world from the ancestral magic war. She had to learn to protect herself better and it was time to contact Dwarf Melmoth!

DEMON GAAP

ONYX & THE VICTORIAN DECK

He was sent to her by forces unknown from a distant land. His land rested against the dramatic canvas of New Mexico's high desert. Where tawny-hued plateaus and expansive blue skies created a beautiful panorama. The land was dotted with crow feathers and juniper trees where the Rio Grande River flowed wildly adding a bloodline to its people and their land. Deep rust-toned ceremonial drums echoed throughout the cliffs like a reverberating pulse of the heart. This land was not just a piece of land-this was a complex web weaved by centuries of turbulent history, rites, and traditions.

One night downcast she was in search of a magical ring that encased a one-million-year-old stone. It was a sea-coloured stone that forms when the heat of lava meets the cool blue waters of the Caribbean Sea. This was an Atlantean Soulmate stone. Swimming in hues of light blue to blue-green, it mimicked the waters of the land it called home. The ring was not only precious but magical! With this ring, she could also control the love spirits.

After aimlessly swiping on the dating app, a message appeared. It was HIM and she knew she had to meet him! By luck he was an alchemist from a long line of jewellery makers and who could easily forge her that magical ring!

He had a unique way with words. A poet. A magician. It was not just his writing; it was his profile. She read his interests and saw they matched her own. The profile was like looking into an old lost friend. The moment their eyes met; she knew he was special. She could feel the sparks fly from their meeting. He stood tall; his chiselled features framed by a cascade of black hair. His warm inviting smile and his eyes, a deep pool of wisdom held hidden stories. With a grace that flowed from his being, he moved with confidence, leaving an aura of strength and tranquillity. His name was Onyx.

They agreed to meet at her favourite restaurant Aqua Arcana. The restaurant was filled with creatures of the sea; lobsters, and urchins, which transported one into an underwater wonderland. The walls were adorned with shimmering abalone shells, red coral, and glowing eels. The ceiling was a vast glass dome, offering a view into the night sky filled with stars, whilst the floor was a gigantic aquarium. The aquarium was home to an array of sea creatures from stingrays and neon tropical fish which darted between colourful corals. In the corner were majestic ocean turtles. Silver dining tables were scattered around, each adorned with clam and sea-cucumber-shaped candles. This was a masterpiece, an offering of an array of seafood delicacies such as mango and octopus carpaccio and steamed lobster tails. At the restaurant, he was the perfect gentleman much more than anyone else she encountered for a long time. Each glance from him felt like a warm embrace.

He took out his Victorian tarot cards from a green velvet pouch and laid them out on the table. He was known for his uncanny accuracy in tarot readings, and Pandora desperately needed his guidance in a time of uncertainty.

As he shuffled the deck, cards flew out with minds of their own and his hands moved with a steady rhythm. He spread the cards out in a fan before her.

"*Choose One,*" he said softly.

Pandora hesitated for a moment before one card whispered to her, and her long fingernail landed on a left card of the spread. He smiled as he turned it over, revealing the Queen of Clubs.

"*The Queen of Clubs,*" he murmured, squinting his eyes. "*This card represents the Mother of Higher Knowledge. Your five of clubs is in Venus. Infidelity, variety of lovers, and sexual indiscretions are not outside your realm,*" he smiled.

He soothed her soul with his voice, and she found herself enchanted, she felt an immediate connection with him. When she met other men, she felt she was just a witch without a wand, lost in the woods. She had never really felt at home with many men to tell them about her magic but meeting him made her feel complete.

What is this feeling I have? It is something I have never felt before. This is what happens when a young man before me becomes a King! She thought to herself.

After dinner she walked him to the train station where they stood in silence, their eyes locked in a bittersweet embrace. The reality of their separation weighed heavily on her heart.

"*I promise to return for you with the ring after I find the stone.*"

"*Until then…remember …Reality is not as serious as it seems. Make light of the game when times are trying. Conscious response dictates One's reality.*" He whispered in her ear.

With a new sense of determination, Pandora left the train station ready to embrace the journey ahead with new hope. As she walked into the night, she carried new wisdom and new truth of the Queen of Clubs, which would guide her every step of the way.

Kanuweia
the Sorceress's
Revenge

In a lush and verdant Polynesian forest on the mystical Island of Borelea, where ancient trees murmured secrets and the ocean teemed with enchantment, Kanuweia came into the world. She was an extraordinary being, part human and part monster witch, imbued with powers that matched those of the revered ancient gods. Kanuweia possessed the unique ability to metamorphose into an orca, a grizzly bear, or a bewitching white moth. When provoked, she could use her delectable food to suffocate her enemies. She was not only Pandora's distant sister but also her dearest friend.

Kanuweia the priestess witch of Borelea; at the age of eleven was sent by the Chief King to a lost grotto where she spent four years on her own to strengthen her magic. At a height of six foot five, she commanded attention, adorned in a striking feathered gown crafted from the plumage of exotic birds like the flamboyant red 'I 'iwi bird, the sleek black 'O'o bird, and the majestic Iwa bird. The dress spoke of her ancestral roots, while her eyes reflected the strength of her forebears, and her voice carried the echoes of ancient, forgotten chants as she navigated the complexities of the modern realm.

Her present life in the magical realm had been one of solitude and sorrow. Long ago, she had been betrayed by men who promised her love and loyalty, only to leave her heartbroken and penniless. Faced with betrayal and consumed by disappointments, she retreated deep into the forest into her mansion, vowing revenge on all who betrayed her.

The witches of her forest were waking up and singing prophetic songs to her:

"Let the moon talk about humans from her point of view,

It is a funny world on the other side of the mirror.

Beware of the Forest Queen, with a taste for human blood!"

With her powerful magic, she crafted a spell that would punish those who wronged her for eternity. She sought out the men who betrayed her and lured them into her forest with promises of a meal and free lodgings, only to ensnare them in her trap.

"Come to dinner, I am cooking tonight, try my witches' casserole and cosmic moon juice!"

One by one, the men fell victim to her vengeance, and with a flick of her finger, she

FIRE
CEREMONY

BIG FEAST

transformed them into ugly dwarves, their once-proud forms were twisted and small, their once handsome faces deformed. Bound by her magic, they became her slaves, forever toiling on her estate from dusk till dawn. But her thirst for revenge was not yet quenched. She continued to seek out those who had wronged her, each new victim adding to the ranks of her dwarf army. There were now seven of such dwarves! She named them: Benevolence, Vanity, Gloom, Envy, Lust, Greed, and Deceit. Each was named after their failings as a prophecy of their fate.

Every night they would prepare for her the most extraordinary feast! The table crawled with an impressive amount of various exotic foods. In the middle of the table stood a Raronka Pigleatus a local wild dangerous boar which only trained warriors could hunt. It was roasted on the pit and stuffed with witches' aromatic herbs and succulent fruits from the Island of Tompai. There were pies stuffed with duck breast and partridge livers with Cognac and sweet leeks. Stuffed Watermelon with minced shark and grouse meat. Fresh oysters with Cajun fruit juice and eels smoked on a forest oak bonfire. As for dessert Coconut pavlova, with grapefruit and passion fruit gelee surrounded with Truffles du Diablo and sherry marmalade. And after the feast, she forced them to dance nude around a large bonfire for the Fire Ceremony until they fell into delirium, and whoever impressed her the most, she would throw a scrap of bread as a reward.

Each night she summoned them to her chamber where she sat on upon her throne of redwood decorated with Kukui nuts and bones. She would listen to their daily tasks and days of labour, judging them and testing if one of them was reformed. Some nights she would smile and other nights a flash of disappointing smile played on her lips.

"And remember, redemption lies in the purity of the soul, your actions, and the sincerity of your hearts. Prove yourselves one day, and you may be free," she said to them.

When the stars came out to play and the evening took the aroma of the night, she would lay in her bed listening to cicadas sing. She loved the softness, the quiet, the sense of rest of her life, and the inviting peaceful dreams. The only thing that she missed was love.

As the years passed, her forest became shrouded in darkness, its once vibrant beauty giving way to a realm of shadows and despair. Few dared to venture into its depths, for fear of falling prey to the sorceress's wrath. However the kingdom of fruits blessed her garden with love hart strawberries and amidst the darkness, there came hope. A young dwarf named Lust had redeemed himself.

Lust was the most subservient and fairest of the dwarves with his blonde locks and ocean blue eyes and his face weathered by years of servitude. He tended to her garden and transformed the once-dead roses into blooming Eden. Once he presented his work to her, a single tear flowed down her face. He looked up at her with pleading eyes. Slowly, he was falling in love with his captor. Kanuweia rose from her throne, her gaze softening as she approached Lust. She laid her large palm on his head and spoke, "*Your heart has proven its worth. Tonight, come to my chambers!*"

Her mansion was built from the remnants of her ancestors' long-standing foes. The mansion's eerie beauty was a twisted marvel, with its exterior ornamented with a chilling pattern of blue bodies, serving as a grim warning to any who dared to approach. The lush forest that enveloped the mansion was teeming with life, from graceful peacocks to gentle donkeys, all amidst the legends and ancient trees that seemed to whisper their secrets to the wind. Inside the mansion, a labyrinth of doors led to seven chambers, each inhabited by her seven slaves, while haunting vines climbed the walls, weaving an intricate web throughout the eerie halls.

As Lust neared her chamber, she solemnly commanded him to venture into the mysterious forest and locate the sacred fire pit. Once there, he was to willingly step into the flames, knowing that only through this act would he regain his original form. "*Go forth! Seek the flames of transformation!*" she urged him with conviction.

As he entered the fire pit, the pain from the flames was intense, making him want to retreat from the fire and flee into the forest. Then he remembered her words and realized that facing the fire was just the beginning of what he needed to do to make amends. The magical fire engulfed him. He watched in awe as his limbs elongated, his features softened, and his stature grew taller. The curse was lifted, and in its place stood a man of striking beauty.

Spying him behind a tree she told him, "*Your transformation is complete. Now you are free to walk and have access to the worlds treasures.*"

But before she could run to embrace and kiss him, she heard Pandora's voice in the rustling leaves.

"My Darling! Spread your wings tonight and fly, sharpen your claws again, and all your wisdom brings, and a new day will begin. True love will come!"

Kanuweia heeded these words with great contemplation and looked at Lust with a mixture of compassion and indifference, and said to him:

"In the universe coded by chaos, the only real thing is love. If I ever give up on love, I have slain myself. With love, I will always find my way home. However, I have come to realize that you, Lust, are not the love that I seek. I know in my heart that I am deserving of a love that is pure, steadfast, and selfless."

Kanuweia gracefully traversed the path leading back to her stately mansion leaving a confused Lust behind in the depths of the forest. A new excitement filled her as she awaited the arrival of her dear friend Pandora, with whom she planned to embark on a much-needed, long vacation.

BACK TO THE FOREST

Pandora realised that her heart remained empty, and her soul was still yearning for a connection that seemed forever out of reach.

One fateful evening, as the moon hung low, Pandora, found herself sitting alone on the floor, gazing at her hands as she traced the lines of her palms. The weight of the silence around her was almost suffocating. Memories of her dead cats and the men she had met, loved and lost flooded her thoughts, leaving behind a profound sense of emptiness. In that solitary moment, she had an epiphany - she had been searching for love in all the wrong places. She had sought validation in the arms of others, hoping they could fill the void within her.

Suddenly she received a message from Dwarf Melmoth through the magic mirror:

"The Queen, is about love! Let go of the pain you have with love. Shift the way you look at things and listen to that silent knowing that your two of cups are to be filled.

Nurture your garden and be with the energy of love and inner beauty. Release your disappointment to the power of the moon.

Trust your intuition and let it guide you into the garden of Venus!"

As she read his message, she delved deep into her own heart, she discovered something she had long overlooked: the unwavering love and friendship she shared with her closest ally, Kanuweia. Who had been by her side from the very beginning, their bond forged and strengthened in the fires of adversity. She was the only person who truly understood Pandora, embracing her for who she was - vampire and witch alike.

With new-found clarity, Pandora made a life-altering decision. She resolved to leave the mortal world behind and return to the magical forest to her friend, her true home. It seemed like the whole world was falling apart, but the forest was falling together. As she stepped through the threshold of the enchanted mirror and into the forest, a sense of peace washed over her, the burdens of her past lifted from her shoulders. She closed her eyes, bidding farewell to her illusions, she was finally home, and she was not dying anymore. She was waiting to be reborn.

THE END